COREY ANN HAYDU

HAND-ME-DOWN MAGIC

STOOP SALE TREASURE

illustrated by

LUiSA URiBE

KATHERINE TEGEN BOOKS
An Imprint of HarperCollins*Publishers*

Katherine Tegen Books is an imprint of HarperCollins Publishers.

Hand-Me-Down Magic #1: Stoop Sale Treasure

For information address HarperCollins Children's Books, a division of HarperCollins Publishers, 195 Broadway, New York, NY 10007.
www.harpercollinschildrens.com
Library of Congress Control Number: 2019951638
ISBN 978-0-06-297825-7 (pbk.) — ISBN 978-0-06-287825-0
Typography by David DeWitt
20 21 22 23 24 PC/LSCH 10 9 8 7 6 5 4 3 2 1
❖

First Edition

For my magical treasure,
Fia Frances
—C.A.H.

For Amelia,
so she can see the magic in herself
—L.U.

ALMA'S NEW
HOME THAT IS
NOT ON A LAKE →

TiTi ROSA, EViE,
AND A LOT OF
LAUGHTER LiVE HERE →

THE HOME WHERE
DEL AND HER FAMiLY
HAVE ALWAYS,
ALWAYS LiVED →

THiS IS WHERE
YOU CAN FiND
LOVE, CREMiTA,
AND ABUELiTA →

THE CURiOUS
COUSiNS
SECONDHAND
SHOPPE →

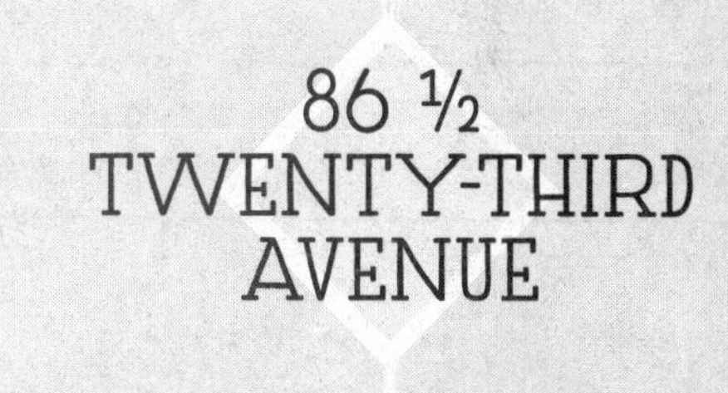

86 ½ TWENTY-THIRD AVENUE

ABUELiTA'S
WiLD AND MARVELOUS
BACKYARD GARDEN

SECONDHAND
SHOPPE

1

86 ½ Twenty-Third Avenue

-Alma-

The Curious Cousins Secondhand Shoppe was located in a brick building with a purple door and flower boxes full of purple pansies at 86 ½ Twenty-Third Avenue. It was Alma's favorite building on the street, but competition was tough. She also loved the bakery that always smelled of cinnamon. She loved the building next door with its stained-glass windows and the one next to that with an enormous flower wreath on its door and a baby-size gnome perched on its stoop.

Alma had been missing Twenty-Third Avenue. She had been dreaming about being right here, with her best friend in the world, her cousin Del. Del's real name was Delfina, but she said that never felt right to her. Del was always the name that fit her best.

"You're here you're here you're here!" Del cried the second Alma stepped out of her parents' old-fashioned green car.

"I'm here I'm here I'm here!" Alma shouted back, and in no time at all, the girls were hugging and screeching and talking so fast that no one else could possibly catch a word of it.

"You two might as well have your own secret language," Alma's mother said with a laugh. "The rest of us don't have a chance of keeping up."

"We should totally invent a secret language!" Del said, missing the point.

"Or learn how to communicate without words!" Alma said. She stared down her cousin. She raised her eyebrows. She stared even harder.

Del stared back, and Alma was sure they were talking through their brains.

Del must have thought so, too, because she exclaimed, "You want a tour of the shop! I heard you! You said you'd been waiting all day to see it!"

Alma still had her polka-dotted suitcase next to her on the sidewalk. She had actually been thinking that she'd like to go up to her new apartment and take a deep breath. She and her parents had driven six hours from their old home on the lake to their new home in the city. Along the way, they had stopped for grilled cheese sandwiches and at a gift shop to buy a frame for the picture Alma had taken of the lake. She wanted to hang it above her bed at her new home, in her new bedroom, above the Curious Cousins Secondhand Shoppe.

But more than that, she wanted to have a best-friend cousin and an awesome first day and a secret no-words language with Del. "Okay," Alma said. "Maybe for a minute."

Every summer, Del spent a month at the lake with Alma and Alma's parents. And every Christmas, Alma spent a few nights with Del and Alma's father's side of the family. There were dozens of cousins and titis and tíos. So many that Alma always lost track when she was trying to count them up.

This would be the first time Alma lived near her whole family. She loved visiting for Christmas, and she loved when Del visited her for the summer. She was pretty sure she would love living here too. But she would miss the icy-blue lake and her big bedroom that looked out at the dock. She loved drawing, and it was especially fun to draw the lake as she admired it from her window. She would miss the fireplace in the living room and how quiet it got at night.

It was very rarely quiet at 86 ½ Twenty-Third Avenue. The first floor was the Curious Cousins Secondhand Shoppe and Abuelita's garden out back, with its huge four-person hammock and dozens of herbs. The second floor was Abuelita's home. Del lived on the third floor with her family. Their cousin Evie and her family lived on the fourth floor with Titi Rosa. Alma and her parents would be moving into the apartment on the fifth floor. She would have to get used to the long walk up the four flights of stairs. She would also have to get used to the hustle and bustle of the city, her nosy little cousin Evie, and enormous family dinners at Abuelita's.

It was a lot to get used to, but Alma was ready. She was almost sure.

2

Fitting In

-Del-

Del was sure that Alma would like the old rocking horse best of all. It was made of worn velvet and squeaked when it rocked. They found it all the way in the back of the store.

"I think the horse is magical," Del said. "I'm pretty sure. Can you feel the magic? I think it belonged to a princess, maybe. Sometimes I think it's trying to talk to me. I bet someday it will ride away, right out of the shop, right out of the whole neighborhood! Don't you think?"

Del was sure her cousin would agree with her. That's what cousins were for, after all.

"It's pretty," Alma said. But she didn't say much else. Del would just have to try harder.

Del showed Alma the basket of scarves and the one dozen jewelry boxes. She showed her where they stored furniture and shoes and coffee mugs. Alma found the display of tiny spoons from faraway countries and cities all over the world. Del had been collecting them for years. Abuelita promised they would go to every spoon city someday.

"Look, it's Paris!" Del told Alma.

Alma's eyes shone, finally. "Is there one for Puerto Rico?" she asked. "I've always wanted to go."

"Of course there is!" Del said. "We found it when we visited last year. Maybe you'll come with us this year!" Del was getting more excited by the minute. There was so much to show Alma!

"This is the accordion. I hope we never sell it,"

Del said, pointing out more of her very favorite objects. She grabbed a bejeweled blue tutu. "This costume was maybe worn by a famous ballerina. It probably was. What do you think? Are these real jewels?"

"Maybe," Alma said. "They're really sparkly. Can we try it on and pretend to be famous ballerinas?"

"Maybe later," Del said. "But first I have to show you the rest of the neighborhood."

"But I've seen the neighborhood," Alma said.

"You live here now! It's totally different!" Del held Alma's hand tightly.

"Oh, okay," Alma said. She sounded unsure. Del would have to think of even more exciting stuff to show her cousin. She pulled her onto the street. Cora and Javi were right outside the door, hanging up posters of Oscar.

"Oh!" Del said, ready to show Alma more things she needed to know about the neighborhood. "This is Oscar! He's very important. He's the best dog on the street. He likes bacon and balls and squirrels. He only barks when he wants to play and when he sees a squirrel."

Alma lit up. Del remembered that Alma loved dogs. "Where is he?" Alma asked his owners. "Can we play with him?"

"He's actually gone missing," Cora said. "He's been gone for two days."

Del gasped. Oscar couldn't be missing. He was such a good dog.

"Will you look out for him?" Javi asked. Del nodded very, very hard.

"We'll find him!" she said. And she really meant it.

"I'm good at finding things," Alma said, and Del remembered the time Alma found her missing stuffed rabbit, Tammy. She could find anything. Alma had moved to Twenty-Third Avenue at the perfect time.

They said goodbye to Cora and Javi and walked all the way up the four flights of stairs to the fifth-floor apartment. Del had decorated it just for Alma, with orange flowers, since orange was Alma's favorite color, and drawings of Alma's old home, and a photograph of the whole family together last Christmas.

"Your new home!" Del said.

"I can't believe I live here now," Alma said. She was smiling and frowning at the same time. Del didn't know that was possible.

"Don't worry," Del said. "I'll help you fit in."

"I don't fit in?" Alma asked. She looked worried, but Del knew there was nothing to worry about. 86 ½ Twenty-Third Avenue was the most wonderful place to live. It was festive and fun and filled with family all the time. She'd get Alma excited about all of it.

"You will!" Del said.

3

Tuesday's Last Customer

-Alma-

"When a customer comes in, always offer them gofio first," Del said. She had been giving Alma lots of instructions about working at the Curious Cousins Secondhand Shoppe. And about their city. And about their family.

Alma listened while she practiced drawing Del's eyes and mouth and nose. She wanted to get her cousin's face exactly right.

"What's gofio?" Alma asked, wishing she already knew.

"Candy made from ground corn!" Evie said, handing Alma an orange roll of paper. Inside was a sugary sweet powder that Alma emptied into her mouth. Evie was always underfoot. Sometimes Alma thought she was alone with Del or with her parents or just with herself, and Evie would pop up to tell her a fact or a joke or to ask for the hundredth time if Alma would play with her.

This time Alma was happy Evie had popped up to tell her something.

"Don't you love it?" Del asked. Alma nodded. It was a new taste and texture. It made her mouth dry. But she liked how sweet it was. And she loved that Abuelita made it herself. "Everyone loves Abuelita's gofio," Del said.

"I do too," Alma said. "Maybe Abuelita will teach us how to make it."

"Great idea!" Del said. "Then when we're grown up we can run a candy store together!"

"With a pet store attached!" Alma added.

"It can have orange walls," Del said.

"I don't like orange," Evie said.

"Alma loves orange," Del said, and Alma thrilled at having a best friend who knew her so well. At the lake, no one ever remembered Alma's favorite color.

"You should try to like purple instead," Evie said. Del smiled. Alma smiled too. Then they both laughed. "What's so funny?" Evie asked. "Purple's not funny! It's pretty!"

Alma was laughing so hard that she didn't notice when a final customer snuck in before they turned the sign from Open to Closed. And when Alma did finally notice, she forgot to offer her gofio.

"Welcome to Curious Cousins!" Del said while Alma stood there forgetting. "Would you like some gofio?"

Tuesday's last customer nodded and took an orange paper cone filled with the candy.

"Welcome to Curious Cousins!" Alma finally said, a little too late. She was trying her hardest to be like Del, but it wasn't easy. Alma knew how to swim in the lake and how to help her mother shovel her long driveway and the name of every kid in her class and all the state capitals. But she wasn't sure she knew how to be a part of her new life and her new family.

"I love your clocks," Tuesday's last customer said. The clocks were Alma's favorite part of the store too. They chirped and rang. They clanged and chimed. They made Alma smile.

So did Tuesday's last customer.

Tuesday's last customer had on a long silver skirt and a rainbow-colored sweater that looked a little like a cape. Dangling from her ears were enormous jangly earrings. They were gold on top and crystal on the bottom, and they looked like chandeliers. Her hair was in three long braids that almost reached her knees.

"She looks magical," Del whispered. Since Alma had arrived two days before, Del had listed at least two dozen magical things. The tree down the block that hung so low over the sidewalk the girls had to duck to get under it. Their titi Rosa's glittery nail polish. Alma's freckled knees. Abuelita's dulce de papaya. The wind chimes in the store's window. Yesterday she even declared the street itself magical. "I bet you've never lived on a magical street," Del told Alma, "but now you do!"

They watched as Tuesday's last customer

picked up objects and put them back down. She looked extra hard at a hippo figurine and an ancient quilt. She considered a tiny lamp with a fancy red shade.

She didn't buy anything.

"More evidence that she's magical!" Del said as they watched her walk out the door. "Magical people come to stores and look at everything and buy nothing!"

"Lots of people do that," Alma said.

"Maybe lots of people are magical," Abuelita said with a shrug. Abuelita had a special way of shrugging. It was one slow shrug followed by one very fast shrug and a lift of her eyebrows.

Del and Alma loved that Abuelita shrug.

"I wonder where she lives," Del said.

Alma had only been living on Twenty-Third Avenue for two days, but she knew what was coming. It seemed that Del was always ready for an adventure while Alma was always ready to slip back into their apartment building and play Guess Whose Footsteps Those Are in the stairwell.

Alma was learning it was hard to say no to adventure-loving Del.

In fact, it was pretty much impossible.

A Belief in Silliness

-Del-

"We have to follow her," Del said. She needed to know more about that mysterious last customer.

"We can't follow a stranger!" Alma said. Del was getting used to Alma saying no. So far, since Alma had arrived, she had said no to dying her hair purple and going to a fortune teller and spending the night in the maybe-magical attic of 86 ½ Twenty-Third Avenue. Del thought the attic was probably a magical place where fairies and elves might visit. Alma thought it was just a dusty old room that made creaky noises and had too many shadows on the walls. Plus, it made her sneeze.

"Well, I'm going!" Del said. She marched right

out the door of the shop. She knew Alma would follow her, and Alma did.

Alma followed behind her, past one dozen posters of missing Oscar and a very busy

ice-cream truck, all the way to the bottom of the street, where they could both see the mysterious woman turn a corner and seem to vanish.

"Oh my gosh, she turned herself invisible!" Del said.

"She's not invisible; she just turned a corner so we can't see her," Alma said.

Del sighed. "You don't get it."

Alma's face fell, and they walked back to the shop in silence. Abuelita met them outside. She put one strong hand on Del's shoulder and one strong hand on Alma's. "I need some help closing up," she said.

"Did *you* think she was magical?" Del asked Abuelita when they were all back inside. Abuelita had kind eyes and black hair and a pretty blue scarf always tied around her neck. Del was proud every time someone said she looked like Abuelita.

Abuelita did her Abuelita shrug. "Maybe we'll find out," she said.

“I bet we will!” Del said.

“Look, I can go invisible too!” Alma said. She ran down the street and hid behind a fire hydrant. “See? Invisible!” she called out, laughing. Del laughed too. Alma might not believe in magic, but she believed in silliness, and that was almost as good.

5

Part-Time Magic

-Alma-

Alma loved empanadas more than almost any food, even chocolate cake.

"We should call them Alma-nadas," Del said.

"What a delicious Alma-nada," Alma's mother said with a smile. She'd tried making them for Alma at their house on the lake, but they weren't as good as the ones Abuelita made.

"More Alma-nadas please!" Evie said. Her plate already had a pile of empanadas. Her mouth was full of them too. But that didn't stop

Evie from reaching for more. Like Del, Evie had lived right here for her whole life. Even she knew more about Twenty-Third Avenue than Alma did.

Alma wished she could live here on Twenty-Third Avenue with her big fun family *and* back at her quiet old home on the lake. She wanted to sit at Abuelita's table and eat empanadas *and* sit on the dock at the house by the lake and skip rocks. She wished she could be in both places, all the time. That would be the best kind of magic.

"We saw an invisible woman today!" Del announced after Alma had eaten her third empanada.

"Me too!" Evie said. Alma smiled at her youngest cousin. Evie just wanted to fit in, like Alma.

"Well now, that doesn't make any sense at all," Titi Rosa said. "How can you see an invisible woman?"

"We saw her before she turned invisible," Del said.

“Ah, so she’s a part-time invisible woman,” Titi Rosa said. She winked at Alma. Alma loved that wink. She tried to wink back, but she was pretty sure it didn’t come out quite right.

“Part-time magic is very common,” Abuelita said. Everyone listened when Abuelita spoke. Alma wondered if she was the only person in her whole family who didn’t believe in magic. At the house on the lake, they never talked about magic. But then, at the house on the lake, it was only ever Alma and her mom and dad, not a whole big family.

"See?" Del said to Alma. "Abuelita believes in magic too. It's part of our family! You'll start believing in it soon, I bet. Don't worry."

Alma's shoulders drooped. There was so much she didn't know about her own family. She wasn't sure if she could ever catch up. She wasn't sure she would ever fit in anywhere at all. Not like Del did.

Titi Rosa shrugged. "I never felt much magic anywhere at all," she said. She winked at Alma again. Titi Rosa had been living on Twenty-Third Avenue for even longer than Del and Evie and Alma had been alive. If it was okay for Titi Rosa not to see magic everywhere, maybe it was okay for Alma too.

6

Stoop-Sale Surprise

-Del-

"Stoop-sale time!" Abuelita said when Del, Alma, and Evie arrived at the Curious Cousins Second-hand Shoppe the next day.

"What's a stoop sale?" Alma asked. Del lit up.

"It's when someone puts all their old stuff on the stairs outside their building—their stoop—and we all get to go look through it and buy the best things."

"Like when we put things we don't want anymore on the stoop?" Alma asked, thinking of books and coats and old toys they had sometimes put outside the building. The objects would always be taken by someone within an hour.

"Sort of. But more official," Del said.

"So, like a yard sale?" Alma asked.

"Sure!" Del said.

"I love yard sales!" Alma said.

"Well then, you'll *really* love stoop sales!" Del said. Del was practically jumping up and down with excitement. That was normal for Del. But she was excited to see that this time, Alma was practically jumping up and down too.

"Why do we go to stoop sales?" Evie asked. She was wearing a sundress and a hat as if she were going somewhere very fancy. Del had told her stoop sales weren't like that, but Evie never listened.

"Good question," Abuelita said. "We go to find special things to share with our customers, with our neighbors."

"Magical things," Del said.

"That's right," Abuelita said. "Magic is meant to be shared. It doesn't belong to any one person. It belongs to us all. And stoop sales are the perfect place to find some hand-me-down magic."

Today's stoop sale was at the end of the block. There was a stoop sale somewhere nearby at least a few times a month.

"Maybe they collect pianos," Del said. Del and Abuelita liked to play Guess What Will Be There when they went to stoop sales. It was a pretty easy game to teach Alma. And Alma was turning out to be very good at it. They walked down their tree-lined street naming possible items.

"Maybe they're selling a bunch of tutus," Alma said.

"Maybe there will be a unicycle," Del said.

"Maybe they'll have moose slippers," Abuelita said. They passed by the little playground with three swings, one slide, and one almost-too-high set of monkey bars. Someone had turned on the sprinkler, and a few kids were running back and forth through water sprouting up from the pavement. Del figured she'd bring Alma there later. Alma would love playing in the water.

"I bet there's a pink umbrella," Alma said.

"A stuffed elephant."

"A golden picnic basket."

They walked by the buildings of Twenty-

Third Avenue. Each building was brick and about the same height. But every building also had something that made it unique. A heavy brass knocker. Flower boxes with orange flowers in the windowsill. Strings of lights hung around the door. Or, in the case of Alma and Del's building, a bright purple door.

"I bet there will be a gallon of silver paint."

"Twenty pounds of peacock feathers."

"A car!"

"A puppy!"

"Maybe it's where Oscar's hiding! Maybe we'll find him there!"

It was fun to guess what might be there, but stoop sales were also serious business. Abuelita trusted Del to pick out the best things from the stoop sale to resell in the secondhand shop. And Del would have to teach Alma all about that responsibility. Sometimes it meant fixing broken things or painting faded things or seeing something special in something that looked boring.

STOOP
SALE!

Today Del was drawn to a huge jewelry box at the top of the stoop. The box itself was pretty: gold satin with little pearls sewn onto the top. But inside was even better. Bangly silver bracelets and long strands of turquoise beads. Huge mood rings and a bunch of friendship bracelets. Del picked out a necklace with a big red stone pendant and a simple gold ring that looked like the one her Dad wore. Alma had found a book of photographs of sunsets and a miniature painting of a bowl of fruit.

"Good work!" Abuelita said when they presented her with their finds. "Now you can pick out something small for yourself."

Del needed to look very carefully through the jewelry box to find the best possible object. She lifted up a heavy gold poodle brooch and looked underneath a velvet pouch that held one single silver button.

Underneath all that was the perfect treasure. A pair of earrings. They didn't look exactly like the earrings belonging to Tuesday's last customer, the part-time invisible woman. But they were similar. They were gold at the top with tiny pink beads hanging from long metal chains. They made the same clinkety-clankety sound the other earrings made. And when Del held them, they made her feel the way Tuesday's last customer had made her feel.

Del didn't have pierced ears. She said it was because she liked her ears just fine the way they were, but really it was because Del's mother didn't think she was old enough. Del's mother didn't think Del was old enough for lots of things. Alma's ears weren't pierced either. Del would have to remember to ask why. It was just one more thing the cousins had in common.

And somehow, as if by magic, these earrings were clip-on earrings. The only kind Del and Alma could wear.

Del clipped them to her ears. They didn't feel light and fake and plasticky the way most clip-on earrings did.

They were heavy and clinkety-clankety and almost certainly magical.

7

Rainbow Pants and a Striped Hat

-Alma-

While Del was looking in a dusty old mirror and Abuelita was measuring a grandfather clock with Evie's help, Alma caught sight of a boy her age across the street.

He stood out because he was wearing rainbow-colored pants and a striped hat that looked like the kind a train conductor would wear. But when Alma saw his face, she scrunched her eyebrows in concern.

When Alma's face looked the way the boy's

face looked, it meant she was sad. And when she felt that way, it helped to talk about it. So Alma approached the boy across the street.

"What's wrong?" she asked. She sat down next to him. From here, the stoop sale looked even more exciting. There was a pile of rugs and three different spice racks. There was a basket of stuffed animals and another of doll clothes. And so many boxes of books. Alma wanted to look at it all. She couldn't imagine anyone being sad, looking at a stoop sale like this one.

But the boy in the rainbow pants and conductor hat was about as sad as anyone Alma had ever seen.

"That's my best friend Ethan Copper's house," the boy said with a sigh. "He's moving away."

Alma knew a little bit about what that felt like. Moving felt like saying goodbye to a part of yourself. It felt like jumping and not being sure when and where you'd land. It felt like you were forgetting some very important thing you had to do, all day long, all the time.

It felt strange.

"I just moved," Alma told the boy. He relaxed a little.

"You did? Do you miss your best friend?" the boy asked. He was near tears. His voice shook.

Alma bowed her head. "No," she said. "My best friend's right there." She nodded toward Del. The boy nodded too. He was a very serious boy, in spite of his not-serious-at-all clothes.

"That's lucky," the boy said.

Alma had been busy feeling left out and confused and sad and worried and excited and awkward. She hadn't remembered to feel lucky too. But the boy was right. Missing a lake was easier than missing a best friend.

8

Oscar and Ice-Cream Sandwiches

-Del-

The good luck started with Del's mother. They ran into her on their walk home when Alma was trying to tell Del about a sad boy with a striped hat. Del's mother was sitting under everyone's favorite tree. The one that hung down very, very low. The tree was a weeping willow that reached so far to the ground that Del and Alma called it a sobbing willow.

"How was the stoop sale?" Del's mother asked.

"It was great!" Alma said. "Look what Del found!"

Del leaned an ear toward her mother. Del's mother didn't usually like the things Del found at stoop sales. So Del waited to hear about how clip-on earrings could hurt your ears or how earrings that big weren't right for little girls to

wear. But instead, Del's mother smiled.

"Beautiful!" she said. "Can I try one?"

Del happily clipped one of the earrings onto

her mother's ear. Like magic, Del's mother lit right up. "I love it!" she said. "A stoop-sale treasure!"

Before Del could say anything, Oscar the dog came bounding up to the girls. Del yelped with excitement.

Even Alma recognized him from the posters hanging up everywhere. "Oscar!" she cried. "We found Oscar!"

"More like Oscar found us!" Del said. Oscar licked her hands and wagged his fluffy white tail. Today was turning out to be the greatest of days.

Alma and Del brought Oscar back to his owners. Javi and Cora were thrilled to see their little dog.

"How in the world did you find him?" Cora asked. Her eyes filled with tears.

"Just good luck, I guess," Alma said.

"Seems more like magic to me!" Del said.

As a reward for finding Oscar, Javi and Cora bought Del and Alma ice cream from the truck outside the park. Usually, the good ice-cream flavors were all gone by this time of day. But today Del and Alma were able to get chocolate-chip-cookie ice-cream sandwiches.

Del's heart was thumping.

For dinner they ordered Indian takeout, and the deliveryman brought an extra order of garlic naan, Del's favorite. While they were washing the dishes, Del's favorite song played two times in a row on the radio.

"Oops, the DJ must have made a mistake," Titi Rosa said when the song started for the second time.

But Del knew it wasn't a mistake at all. She touched the earrings still clipped to her ears.

It had to be magic.

9

Crowns for Queens

-Alma-

Before bed, Alma, Del, and Evie played a game of charades with Abuelita and Titi Rosa. Alma's parents and Evie's parents and Del's parents were all in the garden gossiping, but Abuelita and Titi Rosa were always up for playing a game. In fact, Abuelita and Titi Rosa were being as giggly as Alma and Del sometimes were. Alma loved seeing Abuelita and Titi Rosa laugh like that. They had secret inside jokes just like Alma and Del had.

"You won't ever beat us!" Abuelita said.

"We are the undefeated charades champion sisters!" Titi Rosa said.

"Wait," Alma said, "we play against Abuelita and Titi Rosa?"

"Yep," Del said.

"And we always lose," Evie said. "Right, Del?"

"We *usually* lose," Del said. "But not tonight. Because now we have Alma!" Alma shone with pride. She wasn't sure exactly what her role in her family was, now that she lived here. But helping Del and Evie win at charades seemed like a great start.

"You'll never beat us!" Titi Rosa said. "Because we are the queens—"

"Of charades!" Abuelita finished with a sneaky smile. Abuelita opened up her purse and pulled out two tiaras. They were plastic and shiny.

Titi Rosa let out an excited yelp. She let Abuelita put one of the tiaras on her head.

"You found those at the stoop sale?" Alma asked.

"Who can say?" Abuelita said. "But they were clearly meant for the queens of charades."

"Well then, you'll have to give them to us soon!" Alma said. Del grinned and gave her cousin a high five. Alma was glowing with pride and a feeling of cozy belonging. This is what she had hoped and hoped and hoped for back at the lake house. Plus, she couldn't wait to draw pictures of Abuelita and Titi Rosa in their crowns later.

Abuelita and Titi Rosa jumped to their feet to start their round of charades.

And Alma wondered if maybe *this* was magic.

But it couldn't be. She didn't believe in things like that.

ALMA

Perfect Day

-Del-

In the morning, Del woke Alma up early.

"Cremita time!" she announced. She felt extra jumpy and extra excited. She'd been feeling that way since Alma arrived, but today she was practically on the moon. "Do you know what cremita is? It's like oatmeal but a million times better. Abuelita makes it with cinnamon. You'll love it."

"I know what cremita is," Alma said. Something in Alma's voice sounded a little tired or a little hungry, but that didn't bother Del at all.

"Well, great!" Del said. "I'm in charge of stirring. It's the most important part. You can do it next time if you want."

Alma nodded, and the two girls bounded downstairs.

Abuelita handed Del the big wooden stirring spoon. But Del got distracted looking at her earrings in the shiny metal above the stove, and she forgot to stir.

"Del? I thought you said stirring was the most important part," Alma said.

"Oh no!" Del cried, looking back down at the pot. She expected it to be burnt or lumpy or

sticky. But it was somehow creamy and perfect in spite of her mistake.

On the walk to the playground, Del looked up at a bird chirping in a tree. And she caught sight of something yellow and green and stripy.

"My sweater!" she said. She jumped up a few times, finally reaching a sleeve and pulling it down. "This has been missing for *months*! It's my favorite!"

"I've never seen a sweater in a tree before," Alma said.

"Magic!" Del said. "It's really happening! And listen!" Del did a little dance on the sidewalk. She was staring at her shoes, tapping them and stomping them and making Alma laugh.

"I don't hear anything," Alma said. "I just see my crazy cousin dancing around."

"Exactly!" Del said.

Del explained that all summer her sandals had made a very annoying squeaking sound. But this morning, there was not a single squeak.

At the playground, Del's favorite swing was free, and all the chalk drawings she and Alma and Evie had made the other day were gone—except for Del's drawing of Alma's lake house. The pink chalk home was still there, with a little pink chalk Alma in one of the windows. Alma couldn't stop looking at it.

"Wow," Del whispered. "This is the best day ever!" Del wanted Alma to be excited about her lucky day. She wanted Alma to be the way she was last night—happy to be here on Twenty-Third Avenue together. She had the perfect thing to tell her to get her all excited again.

A secret. Alma and Del loved telling secrets. Just like Titi Rosa and Abuelita were always doing.

"I have a secret," Del said. "I know you don't know anything about magic because you haven't been here for long enough, but these are magic earrings. The earrings are bringing the luck."

11

The Big Fight

-Alma-

"Well, I wouldn't tell anyone that a pair of earrings is bringing good luck," Alma said, "because it's not true." She was getting tired of everything good happening to Del.

"It's definitely true!" Del said. "Look at my hair. It's a whole inch longer. I've been saying I wished my hair would grow longer forever, and it never does. And last night it did!"

Alma looked at Del's hair. It didn't look any longer. Alma was getting *especially* tired of Del acting like she knew everything about everything. Alma knew things too. Alma knew all kinds of things!

"You just *want* the earrings to be magical," she said. "Just like you wanted that lady to be magical. Even Evie knows earrings are never, ever magical." Alma wasn't sure this was true, but she liked sounding sure about it. She wanted to feel sure about *something* in this new life of hers.

Del's face scrunched up. "Maybe you just aren't able to see magic," she said. "Maybe Abuelita and I can see things you can't. Maybe when you've lived with us for longer—"

"You think you know everything," Alma said.

"You think *you* know everything," Del said.

They both crossed their arms over their chests. They both stomped their right foot one time. They both made a *hmph* noise.

Alma and Del didn't look so similar, but sometimes it was very, very clear that they were cousins.

"I'm going home," Del said. "Don't follow me."

"*I'm* going home," Alma said. "Don't follow *me*."

Of course Alma and Del lived in the same building, so they both had to follow each other home. But they didn't speak a word.

12

On the Nightstand

-Del-

Family dinner was at Del's apartment that night. At least fifteen people were coming, since so much of the family lived right on this very street. But Del decided to go to bed early.

"You don't want dinner?" her mother asked. "Titi Clara is bringing lasagna. You love Titi Clara's lasagna." Del loved most everything about family dinner. But tonight that didn't matter.

"We've barely seen you girls!" Alma's father said. Alma's mother and father had been so busy setting up their new home that Del had hardly seen them. They didn't know how mad she was at their daughter.

"You don't even want dessert?" Abuelita asked. She and Titi Rosa were busy making majarete. It wasn't really a two-person job, but they said it was better when they did it together.

"More love that way," Abuelita would say.

"No, thank you," Del said. "I'm tired."

"Must be all that magic," Alma mumbled. Maybe Alma thought Del couldn't hear her, but she could. Del stuck out her tongue. Alma turned to one of her drawings. Del noticed that Alma was always drawing. Del preferred the playground. And maybe since Alma had arrived, Del had made fun of the way Alma could sit in a corner for hours drawing a single face over and over. But it wasn't like the way Alma was making fun of her now. Not at all. That was very, very different.

"You won't even give the earrings a chance," Del said. She thought Alma would be happy to move here. Del had never been happier about anything than she had been about Alma's move. And she thought Alma would be happy about her good luck. She wanted to share it with her, after all. But Alma wasn't sharing in all the happiness. Instead she was trying to ruin it.

"*Clip-on* earrings," Alma said. "I don't have to give them a chance. They're nothing."

This was the meanest thing Del could imagine Alma saying. The earrings weren't nothing. They were *everything*. And if Alma could say something so mean, Del didn't want to be anywhere near her. Even if it meant going to bed a little hungry. Even if it meant missing family dinner.

Tucked into bed way before bedtime, Del tried to sleep in her magical clip-on earrings. But very quickly, her ears started to ache from the weight of them. They were too tight. She thought they might bring her magical, lucky dreams. But in fact, they made it impossible to sleep. Del put them on her nightstand. She watched them until her eyes started to close, and she drifted off.

She couldn't wait to put them on in the morning. And maybe, somehow, the magical earrings would be so lucky that they'd fix what was broken between her and Alma. That would be the best kind of magic.

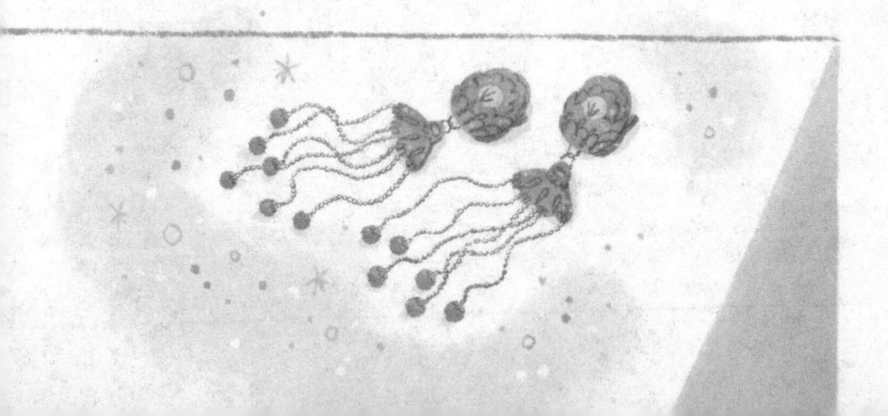

13

An Almost Apology

-Alma-

Alma wanted to apologize to Del. That was her plan. It really, really was. She'd said something much meaner than she'd meant to, after all. And when she thought about the sad boy at the stoop sale missing his best friend, she remembered that a best friend was a wonderful thing to have. She owed it to that sad boy to make up with Del.

But when Alma entered Del's room after dinner, she saw that her cousin was asleep. Alma wasn't sure what to do. Maybe she should leave

Del an apology note.

Alma was about to find a piece of paper and pencil when she caught sight of the earrings. They somehow looked even bigger, even more ridiculous, here on Del's nightstand. They were *so* pink and *so* shiny and *so* over the top.

It was the earrings' fault that she and Del were fighting! It was their fault that Del had skipped dinner and Alma had to try to explain why to her whole family. It was their fault that her first week here hadn't gone as planned.

All of a sudden, Alma was so mad that these ridiculous, over-the-top, crazy-looking clip-on earrings could cause so much trouble. It didn't seem fair. It didn't seem right. And she had to do something about it.

If the earrings vanished, there wouldn't be anything to fight about. Alma and Del could go back to being their usual best-friend-cousin selves.

Alma knew what she had to do. Very quietly,

she reached for the earrings. They were heavier than she thought they'd be. There was a tiny clink and clank. A whisper of a jingle and jangle. Del stirred. But she didn't wake up.

Alma put the clip-on earrings into her pocket and snuck downstairs. They clinked and clanked and jingled and jangled the whole way down, but no one seemed to notice.

Over the years, Alma and Del had put many, many things on their stoop during Alma's visits. It was one of Alma's favorite things to do when she visited Del. They'd put out books they didn't like, sweaters that no longer fit, toys they'd outgrown. Once they even put a whole birthday cake on the stoop, just to see what would happen. It was gone within an hour.

So Alma knew when she put those certainly-not-at-all-magical clip-on earrings on the stoop that someone would want them.

Since they were clip-on earrings, they practically demanded to be clipped somewhere. She clipped them to the ears of the stone lion-head statue that was atop the stone railing of the stoop. She'd never known why it was there or what it meant. But that lion sure looked dressed up now. Ready for a party.

She took one last look at the lion and ran back inside, pretending she'd never been there at all.

14

Nowhere to Be Found

-Del-

Del woke up on the floor with a loud *thump*.

She had never woken up on the floor before. It hurt.

"Ouch!" Del cried. She must have rolled out of bed somehow. Maybe a bad dream.

Maybe just bad luck.

Del rubbed her back and her elbow. It wasn't a good start to the day.

The very next thing that happened was that Del felt a puddle of water beneath her. She looked up and saw the problem immediately. She had left her window open overnight. And there had been a storm. She didn't usually sleep through things like storms. But this must have been a big one. The rain outside had mostly stopped. Inside, though, everything near her window was soaked through. Including Del's favorite stuffed animal, a teddy bear named Oso. Abuelita had given Oso to Del when she was born, and had given him the name to help Del learn Spanish. Del had always loved him.

Oso was a little delicate from being loved for so long, but now he looked positively ready to fall apart from all the water.

It seemed strange, after all that good luck, to have so much bad luck in one morning.

I better put on my magical clip-on earrings! Del thought. *Those will fix things, I'm sure.* She reached up toward her nightstand, but her hands couldn't find the earrings.

And when she looked at her nightstand, there was nothing there.

Del gasped. She sank down to the wet carpet and checked all over for the magical earrings. She looked under the nightstand and under the bed and even over by the door, just in case they were so magical that they could float over there somehow.

But the earrings were not in her room.

Del flew through the building on Twenty-Third Avenue. She asked Titi Rosa and Abuelita and Tío George and even little Evie. No one had seen the earrings. When she knocked on Alma's door, she was ready to explode.

"Have you seen them?" Del asked.

"Seen what?" Alma asked.

"My earrings!"

Alma shook her head. "I haven't seen them," she said.

Even though Del was angry with her cousin, she knew Alma would never lie to her. She and Alma always told each other the truth. That was a very important part of being a best-friend cousin.

Del went onto the street. She asked Uncle Andy, who was often sitting on a lawn chair in front of his building next door, watching the comings and goings of the neighborhood. He shrugged his shoulders. She asked the Goldberg twins, who were walking to the playground. They hadn't seen any earrings. She looked under the beautiful sobbing tree and in the bakery and in every nook and cranny of the Curious Cousins Secondhand Shoppe.

No earrings anywhere.

15

A Big, Big Mistake

-Alma-

Alma was ready to enjoy the earringless, magicless day. But when she found Del on the playground, she could tell it wasn't going to be a normal day. She was starting to think there were no normal days on Twenty-Third Avenue.

Del looked all a mess. She explained to Alma that a bus had driven into a puddle and splashed mud all over her outfit. A bee had stung her cheek, and it was a little swollen. And Del was limping because she'd tripped over a bump in the sidewalk and hurt both of her knees.

Alma's stomach turned a little. She didn't believe in magic, but Del was sure having a string of bad luck this morning.

"Please help me look," Del said.

Del looked so sad and so messy and so lost that Alma had to say yes.

The cousins looked all over the playground for the earrings. Alma almost convinced herself they could be there. At every turn, Del's luck got worse. When she looked by the slide, a toddler coming down fast flew into her. When Del looked in the sandbox she came across a discarded baloney sandwich that smelled simply awful.

When Del looked over by the gate, she accidentally pinched her fingers in the lock.

Alma hated seeing so many bad things happen to Del. Even when they fought, she still loved Del more than anyone in the world.

"This is the worst day of my whole life!" Del

cried. "Nothing's going right!"

Del and Alma walked home, and another bus drove through water, splashing Del *again*. A dog barked at her so loudly that she got scared and had to run away from it. Then she accidentally ran into Mrs. Jones, who lived down the street. Mrs. Jones was carrying a big bag of groceries that went all over the sidewalk. An egg cracked on top of Del's new sparkly red sneakers. And Mrs. Jones scolded Del for being so careless.

Alma had never seen Del look so sad. Del being sad made Alma feel sad.

Alma felt something else too. A little guilty.

Then a lot guilty.

"Now do you believe in the earrings?" Del asked Alma.

Alma wasn't sure what to say. She didn't know what to believe. The one thing she was sure of, though, was that she'd made a big, big mistake.

No More Words

-Del-

Back home, Del went up to her bedroom and closed the door. She felt terrible. After such a perfect, magical day with the dangly gold-and-pink beaded clip-on earrings, she felt absolutely hopeless. She wanted a hug from Oso, but he was still waterlogged and lying out to dry in Abuelita's garden with all the laundry.

There was a knock at her door.

"I don't feel like talking to anyone," Del said.

She was trying not to cry, but it wasn't going very well.

"I have to tell you something," Alma said. Del noticed that she was blushing. She knew her cousin very well. If Alma was blushing, it meant that she'd done something bad.

"What did you do?" Del asked.

Alma did her imitation of an Abuelita shrug.

"What did you do, Alma?" Del asked again.

"I stole and I lied," Alma said.

Del's heart fluttered. Her feet itched. Her nose stung. Her eyes clouded. Her back got wet. Her stomach flipped.

"I stole the earrings. And I told you I didn't know where they were. But I do know." Alma did the Abuelita shrug again. A sad, guilty version of it.

"I put them outside," Alma said. "But then I changed my mind! Really quickly! I went out to get them back, but they were already gone!" Alma's voice was high and fast, the exact opposite of Del's.

"You put. My magical earrings. On the stoop?" Del asked.

"No!" Alma said. "I put them on the lion's ears, actually. He looked really good in them. Distinguished."

Del couldn't find any words. This was bad luck too. She needed to speak. She needed to yell at her cousin. But the words were all gone.

"I don't know why I did it," Alma said.

Del said nothing.

"I was tired of talking about magic," Alma said.

Still, Del said nothing.

"Every day since I've been here, all you do is tell me about magic. And tell me all the things you know and all the things I don't know. I feel left out of my own family." Alma spoke quietly, but Del heard the words as if they were very loud.

Del still didn't know what to say. All she wanted was for Alma to like magic, the way she liked magic and the way Abuelita liked magic. All Del wanted was for Alma to have fun at her new home, and to be excited to be together, just like Del was.

"No one talked about magic at my old home," Alma said.

For the first time, Del realized Alma might miss her old home. Maybe Alma was happy to be here *and* sad sometimes too.

"I don't know anything about it. Or anything about the shop. Or anything about our family, I guess."

Alma looked a little sad and a little lost. Del

didn't want her to be either of those things, but she was still mad about the earrings. And she was pretty sure she was getting a cold. And her foot was falling asleep. And clouds were coming in, ruining the day even more. And it was all Alma's fault.

Del finally had something to say. But she needed to say it to Abuelita.

17

Curious Cousins

-Alma-

Alma didn't like the way Abuelita was looking at her.

"She stole my earrings! She gave them to a lion! A stone lion! Not even a real one!" Del said. "Then she lied about it!"

"And has the lion been lucky?" Abuelita asked.

Alma and Del hadn't thought to check. They looked out at their building's stoop. The lion head was there, as usual. It was pretty hard to tell if a stone lion was lucky or not.

"Probably," Del said. "Since it had the earrings."

"I wonder what a stone lion considers lucky," Abuelita said.

"Maybe someone dropping ice cream on its face?" Alma asked. "So it could get a taste?"

"Or someone planting nice-smelling flowers right under its nose?" Del suggested.

"Someone putting another lion head across the street so it has someone to hang out with?" Alma said. She was starting to giggle.

"Someone bringing a real live lion by!" Del said.

"Yes!" Alma exclaimed. She was getting excited by these ideas. This is what she and Del were best at. Coming up with ideas, making jokes, imagining funny or fantastic things. It's what they always did during their summers together at the lake house. It's why they were best friends.

"Wait," Del said. "That's not the point. The

point is Alma did something wrong, and she has to get in trouble."

"Ah," Abuelita said. But she didn't send Alma to her room or tell Alma she'd been bad. Alma didn't know what to make of it.

"I made a mistake," Alma said.

"A huge mistake," Del said. "A mean mistake."

"You know," Abuelita said. "Your titi Rosa and I had a hundred fights like the one you two are having."

"You did?" Alma asked. It was hard to imagine Abuelita and Titi Rosa fighting. They were best friends. They had started the Curious Cousins Secondhand Shoppe together. They finished each other's sentences. Sometimes they laughed so hard that the whole neighborhood seemed to rumble and shake with their joy.

"We sure did," Abuelita said. "About magic."

"Titi Rosa hated magic too?" Del asked. Alma wanted to say how unfair it was to say it like that, but she kept her mouth shut. She was the one who had stolen and lied, after all.

Abuelita chuckled. "I used to see it that way," she said. "But that's not quite right, is it, Alma?"

Alma shook her head. "It's not right at all! I don't hate magic! I just don't— It doesn't seem— I don't see it everywhere like you do. I don't really—"

"You don't understand it," Del said. Alma loved that Del knew how to finish her sentences. Maybe not as well as Titi Rosa could finish

Abuelita's. But close.

"I guess I'm curious about it," Alma said. "When I'm not mad about it."

"I'm curious about it too," Del said.

On that they could agree, at least.

18

Belonging

-Del-

Del wasn't ready to forgive Alma completely, but she was ready to talk to her.

"Do you believe a little bit?" she asked her cousin while they sat in the backyard sipping Abuelita's famous lavender lemonade. Del was pretty sure the lemonade was magical too.

And there was no denying that the clip-on earrings had brought luck, as far as Del was concerned. She had been lucky when she wore them and very, very unlucky when they were gone.

How could Alma not see how totally real magic was? Would she start to believe, the longer she lived here?

"I don't know what I believe," Alma said. "But I like the way you believe. And I like the way Abuelita believes. And maybe someday I could believe too."

"Really?" Del asked.

"I've never seen so much bad luck in my whole life!" Alma said. "So maybe there's something to those earrings after all. Maybe if I'd lived here my whole life like you—"

"Then you wouldn't be you," Del said.

"But I'd be more part of the family," Alma said.

"You're already a part of the family." Del said. "You always have been. Even when you lived on the lake."

"Even though I don't know all the jokes and rituals and everything about stoop sales and magic and the city and cremita?" Alma asked.

Del nodded. "Of course. Plus, you're a

stoop-sale natural." Del saw Alma's smile, and it was the best, biggest smile she'd seen from her cousin since she'd arrived. This whole time, Del had thought her job was to tell Alma all about her new home. She hadn't realized that what Alma really needed was to be told she belonged there.

And of course she did. She belonged right here, next to Del, drinking lavender lemonade.

19

Not a Unicorn, Not a Mouse

-Alma-

Alma and Del had just finished their lemonades when they heard the noise. It was a scuttling and breathing and rustling sound.

"Do you hear that?" Alma asked.

"Must be magic afoot," Del said. Maybe Del was always going to think everything was magical. But Alma was pretty sure the sound was coming from the garden. Maybe a mouse. But it was too loud for a mouse. Maybe Oscar had gotten off his leash again and escaped into their backyard. She wondered if he'd done that before. But Oscar always barked at squirrels when he was outside, and she didn't hear any barking.

Alma got up and looked around their little backyard. There were all of Abuelita's beautiful flowers and all of Titi Rosa's vegetables and herbs. There was a discarded picnic blanket in one corner and a worn lounge chair in the other. Alma nudged Del. She pointed at the picnic blanket. At first Del looked confused. But then she saw what Alma had seen. A little bit of movement under the blanket.

"A raccoon?" Alma suggested.

"A unicorn?" Del said.

"A squirrel?"

"A fairy?"

They went back and forth, Alma naming animals, Del naming magical creatures, and it looked like they might start fighting again, as their suggestions got more and more spirited. It was right after Alma suggested a bunny and Del insisted it must be an elf, that the picnic blanket flew up in the air and revealed what kind of creature was actually underneath.

It was a cousin.

They should have known.

It was little Evie, hiding underneath the picnic blanket, listening to her big cousins.

"What in the world were you doing under there?" Alma asked.

Evie shrugged. It was a little like an Abuelita shrug and a little like an Alma shrug and a little bit like her very own kind of shrug.

And after the shrug, she opened her eyes wide and stuck her hand into her pocket and pulled out one pair of gold-and-pink dangly clip-on earrings.

20

No One and Everyone

-Del-

Del hadn't thought she'd ever see those earrings again. And certainly not from Evie.

Del lunged for her magical pink-and-gold dangly earrings. Alma gasped.

Evie closed her hand tightly around them. "You can have them back," she said. "But only if you don't have any more fights. Not ever again."

"Evie Maria," Del said. It was very serious when they used each other's full names. "You give those back right now. They're mine."

"Delfina Ann," Evie said, every bit as serious, "Abuelita said magic doesn't belong to anyone."

Del stopped her lunging. Alma's mouth stayed open. Evie had said something that even her big cousins had to stop and think about.

They *had* heard Abuelita say that before. The day of the stoop sale. Abuelita said that magic doesn't belong to any one person. Magic belongs to everyone. And no one.

Alma and Del sat down. They had to sit down to think. Evie sat down too. She wasn't thinking, but she liked copying what her cousins did.

"She's right," Del said. "The best kind of magic is hand-me-down magic."

21

Felix Sanderson's Lucky Day

-Alma-

Even though it had been a few days since the stoop sale that started it all, Alma couldn't stop thinking about one thing. One person, actually.

"Evie," she said after thinking it through, "who is Ethan Copper's best friend?" Ethan Copper was the boy who was moving away from the neighborhood with his family. Alma knew his best friend would be the sad boy who had watched her at the stoop sale.

"Oh that's easy," Evie said. "Felix Sanderson."

"Felix!" Alma exclaimed, much to her cousins' confusion.

"Who is Felix Sanderson?" Del asked.

"A boy I know," Alma said.

"From the lake?" Del asked, all turned around and confused.

"He's not from a lake!" Evie said. "He lives at the bottom of the street!"

"And he's best friends with Ethan Copper, who moved away?" Del asked. Alma watched as Del thought about it. Del's face made a lot of movements when she was thinking. Her eyes squinted and her nose wrinkled and her mouth flipped up and down from mini-smile to mini-frown.

"I would hate if my best friend moved away," Del said at last. "Even though she hasn't lived here for very long at all." Del grinned. It made Alma grin too.

"I would hate that too," Alma said. "I like having my best friend live so close."

They looked very hard at each other. Alma knew they were both thinking the same thing. They didn't need any more luck. They were already the luckiest people on all of Twenty-Third Avenue. Maybe they were the luckiest people in the world. Because from now on they would always be two floors away from their best friend.

"I bet Felix Sanderson could use some luck," Del said.

Alma didn't give an Abuelita shrug to that. She gave a big, enthusiastic Alma nod. "He could maybe even use some magic," she said.

Del and Alma and little Evie walked down Twenty-Third Avenue. They passed by the sobbing tree with its drooping branches. They waved to Cora and Javi playing with Oscar in the park. They saw Titi Clara and Uncle Andy on their stoops, calling to each other across the street. They passed by all the brick buildings with all their special details. Year-round Christmas lights around one building's window. A bright green birdcage hanging from one neighbor's tree. A polka-dotted doorknob and a knocker shaped like a giraffe. They walked by every wonderful bit of the street.

And like magic, at the very end of Twenty-Third Avenue, they found Felix Sanderson right

where they thought he might be. Sitting across the street from the Coppers' building, watching the new neighbors move in. He had striped shorts and a pink shirt and over that a brown vest, like the kind Alma's father had worn to her cousin Flor's wedding. Alma liked that Felix Sanderson didn't dress like other people she knew.

Evie waved at him. Evie was good at waving at people. She loved being friendly. Felix waved back. He looked like he could use some friendliness.

"We have something for you," Alma said. She did an Abuelita shrug.

"It's something magical," Del said.

Alma didn't contradict her cousin. She just clipped an earring onto Felix's vest. It was a pretty fancy vest, so the earrings made sense there. Del clipped the other one on.

Maybe some people would think it was strange, to have magical earrings clipped onto their clothes. But not Felix Sanderson. He smiled. He had been wishing for some friends. And it seemed he had come into a little bit of luck at last.

Acknowledgments

It has been a pure joy to work on this book, and so many people added to that joy.

Many thanks to my agent, Victoria Marini, for making it happen.

Thank you to my editor, Mabel Hsu, for heaps of creative insights, bundles of care and thought, and for loving my characters with me.

Thank you, Katherine Tegen, for years of support as I find new kinds of stories I want to tell.

A very special thank-you to incredible illustrator Luisa Uribe. You truly made Alma, Del, and their neighborhood come to life, and I'm so grateful for your big-hearted, beautiful illustrations.

Thank you so much to Alexandra Hernandez,

Bianca Vargas, Kayla Ruiz, Nivia Scallon, and Frank Scallon for reading, answering questions, and helping me make Alma and Del's world sparkle.

Thank you to the smart, thoughtful, and talented bookmakers, book lovers, book designers, and book collaborators who helped me turn this story into a book on a shelf and add a dash of magic to everything I do: Alexandra Arnold, Tanu Srivastava, Amy Ryan, Alexandra Rakaczki, Maya Myers, Allison C. Brown, David L. DeWitt, Emma Meyer, Sam Benson, and Robert Imfeld.

And a heartfelt thank-you, thank-you, thank-you to the Haydu, Scallon, Maldonado, Olavarria, Borrero, Ross, and Spokes families. This is a book about family, and mine has always been bookfilled and cozy and is also newly big and boisterous, and it all makes me smile.

Alma and Del's magical mishaps and fun continue in *Hand-Me-Down Magic #2: Crystal Ball Fortunes.*

Read on for a sneak peek!

1

Delightful and Daring

-Del-

There were only sixteen hours to go before Del's Delightful and Daring Dress-Up Party. She had been counting down the hours for an entire week. Everyone participated in the countdown because Del loved birthdays and Abuelita loved hosting parties and the whole family loved cake and party hats and singing one round of "Happy Birthday" followed by one round of "Feliz Cumpleaños" at the top of their lungs.

"How many people are coming?" Alma asked.

She was putting together goody bags for the guests. She'd helped Del pick out stickers and sparkly pens and three different kinds of chocolate. "This seems like a lot of chocolate." She gestured to the enormous pile. Their littlest cousin, Evie, couldn't stop eyeing it. It was so tall that Alma couldn't see over the top of it from her seat at Abuelita's kitchen counter. It was so tall that Evie had named it Chocolate Mountain and said they should keep it just like that forever.

"Like, a million people," Del said. "Pretty much everyone ever. And they're all going to be dressed up! I can't wait to see what they're all wearing!"

"A million?" Evie repeated. She was bouncing up and down on her toes. "Really?"

"No, not really," Del said. She rolled her eyes at Alma. But Alma looked nervous, like she thought there really might be a million people shoved into Abuelita's apartment tomorrow, too. "More like twenty. But still. That's a lot. That's more than were at my party last year. But I'm going to be another year older, so it makes sense."

"Twenty is a lot less than a million," Evie said, huffing. "You're not very good at math, Del."

"Not as good as you, I guess," Del said, laughing.

Evie thought about this. "Do you think I'm good enough at math to count all these chocolate bars?" she asked.

"Why don't you try?" Del said. Evie started counting pieces of chocolate very loudly. So loudly, in fact, that Abuelita and Titi Rosa came into the kitchen to see what all the fuss was about.

Abuelita made a startled noise—"Oh!"—and smiled. Del and Alma turned to see what she was looking at. She was facing the window that looked out at the backyard. And right there, perched on the birdbath, was a little black kitten. She was dipping her paws into the birdbath, then shaking them off, over and over, like she was trying to figure out something very important.

"What a darling gatito!" Abuelita said. "¡Hola, mi gato!" she called out to the kitten.

The kitten jumped in surprise, and the jump made her stumble all the way into the birdbath with a cute kitten-y splash. Del thought the kitten might be scared, taking that fall. But instead she seemed interested in the water. She licked it. She pawed at it. She jumped out of it, then right back in.

Del had seen a lot of stray cats before, but never one that acted anything like this one.

"It's time to start winding down," Titi Rosa

said, directing them away from the window and the now-very-wet kitten.

"But we have so much decorating left to do!" Del said.

"And so much chocolate to eat— I mean count!" Evie said.

"I've never been to a delightfully daring dress-up party," Alma whispered to Del. She sounded nervous.

"Don't be a fraidycat!" Del said. "This party is going to be perfect."

"I hope so," Alma said. "And I'm not a fraidy-cat. I just get scared of new things sometimes."

"How can you be scared when you're going to be wearing this!" Del ran to the closet where she'd been storing her big surprise: two big fluffy boas. They'd been planning their costumes for the party for a while, but this would be the perfect addition, Del was sure. She wrapped the orange boa around Alma and the blue one around herself.

"What can go wrong when you have a boa?" Del asked. She twirled her blue boa and did a little birthday dance.

Alma pulled her boa more tightly around herself.

"Trust me," Del said. "Tomorrow will be the best day ever."